WASHOE COUNTY LIBRARY

3 1235 03517 5616

P9-ECN-846

Happy 100th Day!

FOR ANGUS, MY GREATEST TEACHER –S.M.

FOR PATRICK X AND LUKE –M.N.D.

Text copyright © 2011 by Susan Milord
Illustrations copyright © 2011 by Mary Newell DePalma
All rights reserved. Published by Scholastic Press, an imprint of Scholastic Inc.,
Publishers since 1920. SCHOLASTIC, SCHOLASTIC PRESS, and associated logos are trademarks
and/or registered trademarks of Scholastic Inc.

No part of this publication may be reproduced, stored in a retrieval system, or transmitted in any form
or by any means, electronic, mechanical, photocopying, recording, or otherwise, without written permission
of the publisher. For information regarding permission, write to Scholastic Inc., Attention: Permissions Department,
557 Broadway, New York, NY 10012.

Library of Congress Cataloging-in-Publication Data
Milord, Susan.
Happy 100th day! / by Susan Milord ; illustrated by Mary Newell DePalma. — 1st ed.   p. cm.
Summary: Graham Elmore hates school, but as the year progresses toward the day
that is both his birthday and the hundredth day of school, Graham's reading improves,
and so does his outlook.

[1. Schools—Fiction. 2. Hundredth Day of School—Fiction. 3. Books and reading—Fiction.
4. Birthdays—Fiction.] I. DePalma, Mary Newell, ill. II. Title. III. Title: Happy one hundredth day.
PZ7.M6445Ham 2011   [E]—dc22   2010009848
ISBN 978-0-439-88281-1
10 9 8 7 6 5 4 3 2   11 12 13 14 15

Printed in Singapore   46

First edition, January 2011
Book design by Elizabeth B. Parisi

Happy 100th Day!

By SUSAN MILORD

Illustrated by
MARY NEWELL DePALMA

Scholastic Press / New York

1st Day
Back to school.

The year just started, but Miss Currier
    is already talking about the 100th day.
We're going to make a paper chain to count the days we're in school.
When the chain has one hundred links, we'll throw a big party.
"100th Day will be one day you'll never forget!" Miss Currier said.

I hate school, and I'm sure not looking forward to the 100th day of it.

3rd Day

Miss Currier is really big on reading.

Reading is the number one reason I hate school.

I can't keep the letters straight, and all the sounds get jumbled up.

When it was my turn, Miss Currier asked me to speak louder.

That just made it worse.

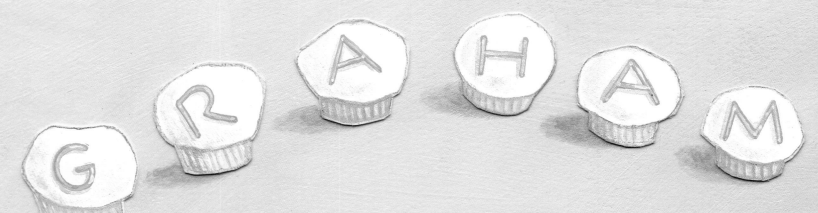

Things got a little better in the afternoon.
We played Pin the Smile on the Clown and arranged tiny cupcakes to make words.
I spelled the one thing I never get wrong—my name.

It turns out Miss Currier is really big on birthdays, too.
At least I have *something* to look forward to.

12th Day

Reading is really hard.
I don't get short vowel sounds and long vowel sounds.
And why are some letters silent?
I must be a dummy, because I don't understand any of this.

Today Miss Currier gave each of us a 100th Day project.
Annabelle is going to write one hundred poems about animals.
Noah will learn one hundred facts about outer space.
Kyle gets to keep a weather log.

I have to read one hundred books.
This is going to be a disaster.

Monday   Tuesday

school days

1   2   3

17   18   19   20   21   22   23   24   25   26   27   28

42   43   44   45   46   47   48   49   50   51   52   53

69   70   71   72   73   74   75   76   77   78   79   80

91   92   93   94   95   96   97   98   99

100

22nd Day

Miss Currier talks about 100th Day a lot.
She says it's the busiest day of the whole year.
There will be classroom stuff in the morning,
    and an all-school assembly in the afternoon.
Today she told us the date.

That's my birthday!
But wait . . . that's 100th Day?

I asked Miss Currier if there would
be time for my birthday party.
"We'll have to see," she said,
but her eyes said *I don't think so.*

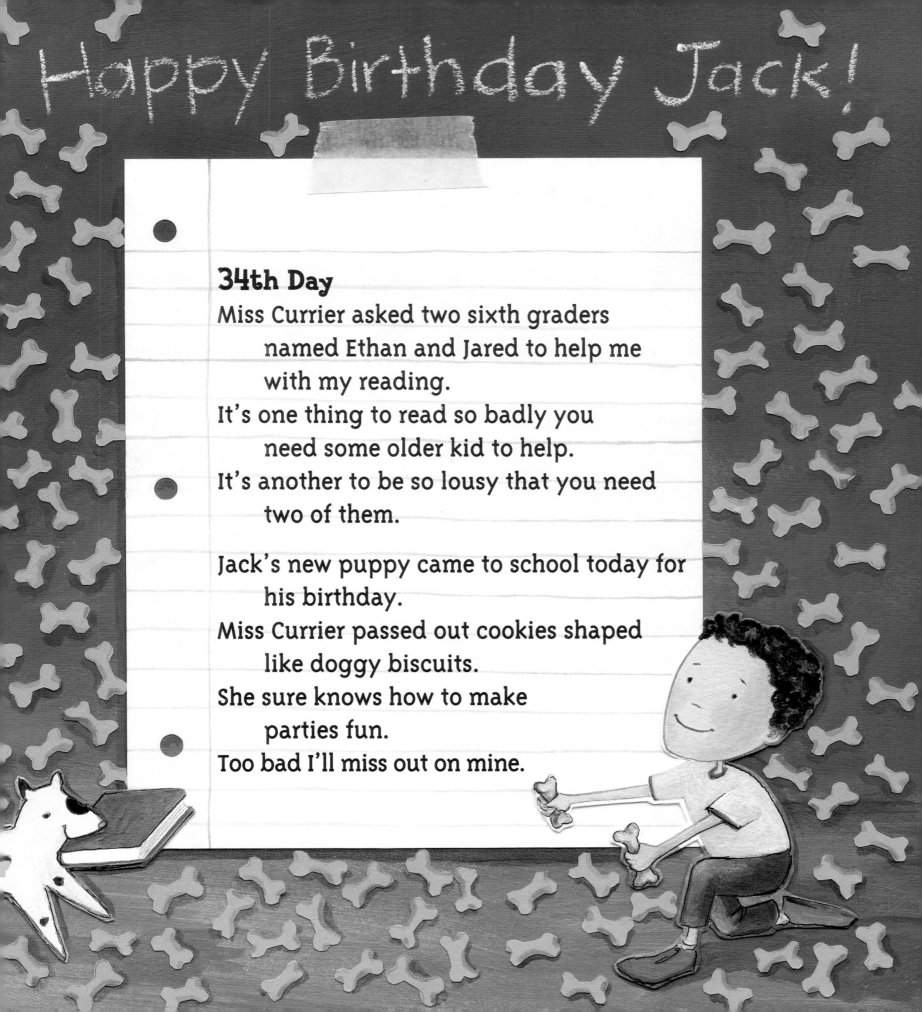

Happy Birthday Jack!

34th Day

Miss Currier asked two sixth graders
    named Ethan and Jared to help me
    with my reading.
It's one thing to read so badly you
    need some older kid to help.
It's another to be so lousy that you need
    two of them.

Jack's new puppy came to school today for
    his birthday.
Miss Currier passed out cookies shaped
    like doggy biscuits.
She sure knows how to make
    parties fun.
Too bad I'll miss out on mine.

42nd Day

We've been counting to one hundred by ones,
    fives, tens, and twenties.
Today we learned how to count by twenty-fives.
Miss Currier showed us how twenty nickels, ten
    dimes, and four quarters each make a dollar.

I laid a quarter, a nickel, and four pennies
    in front of Miss Currier.
"This is how many books I've read so far,"
    I told her.

Ethan joked about paying me for every
    book I finish.
Jared said if they did that, they'd go broke.

Happy Birthday to Darren and Karen!

58th Day
This afternoon we had a birthday party for Darren and Karen.
They're twins, so Miss Currier split our class into pairs to play
    Rock, Paper, Scissors.
We made special treats using two cookies and ice cream.
Of course, we counted to one hundred by twos.

Today I read a book without any help.
Miss Currier didn't seem surprised, but I sure was.

66th Day

I'm working really hard at reading.
Ethan's stopped coming, and Jared helps
    only twice a week now.
I've finished as many books as there are
    links in our chain.

I never thought I'd read this many books
    in my whole life.
But I still don't know how I'll complete
    one hundred of them in time.

73rd Day

Our paper chain stretches from one end of the classroom clear to the other.

We celebrated Delia's birthday today.
Miss Currier twisted balloons into different animal shapes.

We ate animal crackers and listened to *Peter and the Wolf*.
I could even read the names of some of the instruments:
    clarinet, oboe, and—my favorite—bassoon.

But I still wish I could celebrate my birthday at school.

87th Day

We've been learning what our town was like one hundred years ago.
We read aloud from diaries kept by kids back then.
When I looked up after my turn, everyone was staring at me.
I didn't stumble on a single word!

Miss Currier asked us to imagine what our town will be like
in another hundred years.
Marc thinks people won't drive cars.
Stephanie worries people will no longer read books.
Jodie doesn't think much will change.
There will still be school.

That wouldn't be so bad, I guess.

Happy Birthday Ruth!

95th Day

It's 100th Day this and 100th Day that every day now.
Each morning, we practice the song we'll sing at assembly.
Each afternoon, we work on getting ready for the big day.

Miss Currier asked everyone to bring in something
      for our 100th Day self-portraits.
I brought a box of regular old pasta.
Everyone is excited about 100th Day.
Everyone but me.

And you know the worst part?
Even though we were really busy today,
      there was still time to celebrate Ruth's birthday.

100th Day

We finally made it.

We jumped right into 100th Day activities.
First, we shared our projects.
I read the titles of all the books I finished.
All one hundred of them.

At recess, we counted how
    many times we could skip rope
    in one hundred seconds.

Then we headed back indoors
    to make one hundred snowflakes
    for our winter mural in the hall.
There was so much going on,
I almost forgot it was my birthday.

But then I remembered.

For my self-portrait, I used forty
    pink sequins, twenty-six pasta
    shapes, two blue buttons, eleven
        split peas, twelve fuzzy balls,
        and nine pieces of straw.

Graham

The assembly started right after lunch.
Each class performed a special 100th Day piece.

Then our principal walked onto the stage.
"Happy 100th Day, everyone!" Mrs. Hannah said.
"Those were amazing performances!
I am so proud of you and all the hard work
    you've put in since school started."

"But today is not just 100th Day,"
    Mrs. Hannah continued.
"Someone in our school has a birthday.
So let's celebrate all your good work
    and Graham Elmore's special day!"

Miss Currier asked me to stand while the whole
    school sang "Happy Birthday."
I got to have the first slice of cake . . . and an
    extra scoop of ice cream.

Miss Currier was right.
This was one day I'll never forget.

Count to 100:

	Pages
paper strips	6-7
letters	8-9
clown smiles	10-11
books	12-13
numbers	14-15
cookies	16-17
10 x 10 20 x 5	18-19
50 2 s	20-21
notes	22-23
words	24-25
pasta	26-27
stars	28-29
snowflakes	30-31
20 x 卌	32-33
students	34-35
links in paper chain	36-37

52

82 79 60 53 93

78 62 94

80 85

65

68

56

83

81 88 52

84 95

59 51